Shinega's Village

PUBLISHED UNDER THE AUSPICES OF THE NEAR EASTERN CENTER
UNIVERSITY OF CALIFORNIA, LOS ANGELES

SCENES OF

BERKELEY AND LOS ANGELES 196

Sahle Sellassie

TRANSLATED FROM CHAHA BY
Wolf Leslau

ILLUSTRATIONS BY
Li Gelpke

Shinega's Village

ETHIOPIAN LIFE

UNIVERSITY OF CALIFORNIA PRESS

UNIVERSITY OF CALIFORNIA PRESS
BERKELEY AND LOS ANGELES, CALIFORNIA
CAMBRIDGE UNIVERSITY PRESS
LONDON, ENGLAND

© 1964
BY THE REGENTS OF THE UNIVERSITY OF CALIFORNIA

SECOND PRINTING, 1966

LIBRARY OF CONGRESS CATALOG NUMBER: 64-12607

PRINTED IN THE UNITED STATES OF AMERICA

TRANSLATOR'S PREFACE

This is the first Ethiopian novel to be published in English. Ethiopia, a land of ancient civilization attested by inscriptions going back to the fourth century of our era, has not contributed any original literary documents to world literature. True, there exists a literature written in Gheez, the ancient language of Ethiopia, but this literature is mainly religious in nature and for the greatest part is translated from other languages such as Greek, Coptic, Syriac, and Arabic. It is only in recent years that Amharic, the national language of Ethiopia, has produced writings of literary value. Novels, dramas,

v

and poetry are now written in that language, but these remain unknown to the Western world for they have not been translated into Western languages. There are some writings in the other Ethiopian languages, such as Tigre, Tigrinya, and Harari, languages that like Amharic belong to the Semitic group; but these writings are also religious in character and are mostly translations. There is, of course, a folk literature in these languages, but it is mainly oral and the few publications are the work of Western scholars.

One of the Semitic languages spoken in Ethiopia is Guragé. This is a language cluster spoken by a distinct ethnic group. The Guragé live in the region south of Addis Ababa, the capital of Ethiopia. There is a great variety of dialects in Guragé, one of them being Chaha. The Chaha speakers are partly Christians of the monophysite type, partly pagans, and partly Catholics, the latter being centered around Indibir, the seat of the Catholic mission. The family of the hero of *Shinega's Village* are Catholic. Chaha has no literature and has never developed an alphabet of its own. The only written documents in the dialect are a catechism written in the Amharic script and texts collected by Western scholars.

This gap now is being filled in part by the original text of *Shinega's Village,* written by Sahle Sellassie, a speaker of Chaha. Being interested in the investigation of the various Guragé dialects, I suggested to Sahle that he describe, in Chaha, the life in his village. At that time he was a student in Political Science at UCLA. He was able to devote the summer of 1962 and several months of the academic year to writing this novella thanks to fellowships granted him by the Near Eastern Center and the African Studies Center of UCLA. The script used was Amharic. Since this script is inadequate for the presentation of all the Chaha sounds, however, the author and I had to devise certain special characters for those Chaha sounds not existing in the other language.

The novella here presented in English is a free translation of the original text. The Chaha text, in the native script, transcribed into phonetic symbols, and accompanied by an exact translation, will be published at a later date.

WOLF LESLAU

Los Angeles, 1963

INTRODUCTORY NOTE

I wrote *Shinega's Village* in the summer of 1962 when I was a graduate student at the University of California, Los Angeles. The book was intended for the eyes of only one reader, Professor Wolf Leslau, Chairman of the Department of Near Eastern and African Languages at UCLA, who desired to have a Guragé text he could refer to in his research. When I finished the story, Professor Leslau suggested that it should be published in English translation. As I had had no intention of writing for the public, and at that for a Western public, I was surprised, but at the same time I could not but be pleased.

The Guragé people number less than one million
and are the descendents of a military colony of Northern
Ethiopians who moved south centuries ago and settled
in central Ethiopia about a hundred miles from Addis
Ababa. Their countryside is a plateau crossed by rivers
that fill during the rainy season; the people are settled
in villages surrounded by farms, and they live by culti-
vating the land and by breeding cattle. The *esset* plant,
or false-banana, as it is called in this book, is the Guragés' staple. They use it not only for food but also for
making rope, for weaving mats, and—the leaves—as a
wrapping-material. They rarely know starvation, for the
esset grows well even when rain is not abundant. Cattle
are also very important to these people, and are treated
with great respect by them, because without meat, milk,
and cheese, *wusa*-bread cannot be fully enjoyed.

As will be clear from the book, modernity has already broken into the traditional life of the Guragé.
Formerly a Guragé would never leave his land and go
elsewhere, except when—as in the case of a murderer—
cursed and exiled, a rare happening. But today a con-
siderable segment of the population lives in the various
towns and cities of Ethiopia, especially Addis Ababa
and Jimma. The chief reason for this is that as the population grows, there is less and less land for cultivation.
Moreover, the cities offer cash wages, not always to be
found in the villages. About fifteen years ago, when I
began my education, there was much reluctance on the
part of parents to sending their children to school. It
was not so much that they disliked education, as that
they loved tradition. Today this trend has reversed, and
every family wishes its children educated, in order to

improve the children's opportunities and also the lives of the parents who depend upon the children.

As *Shinega's Village* was written in Chaha, the first book in the history of the dialect, it could not be very sophisticated. If I had used English, or for that matter Amharic, I could have enlarged the scope of the book and made it appear more modern. But undoubtedly the spirit I wanted to convey would have been lost.

I would like to point out, furthermore, that *Shinega's Village* presents facets of only *one* aspect of Ethiopian life. If one should go to the northern or southern provinces, not to mention the cities, one might not find the kind of life described in this little book. For Ethiopia is a country with diverse customs, traditions, religions, and languages.

SAHLE SELLASSIE

Los Angeles, 1963

1   SHINEGA'S BIRTH

In the village of Wardéna it was evening. A fire of dry olive wood burned without smoke in the open fireplace in Bala's house, flickering and casting shadows upon the round walls. Small calves, hungry for their mothers' udders, bawled in the stable part of the room, for it was time for the cowherd to drive the village cattle home. In Bala's house the lowing of the returning cattle could be heard.

While Matebet, the maid-servant, rinsed the kettle to prepare evening coffee, Bala's wife lay on a mat near the fireplace warming herself. She did not feel well;

she was far gone in pregnancy, and the birth of the child was expected tonight or tomorrow. Bala sat on the left side of the door, the lower half of which was closed, in the *kakat,* the part of the big room reserved for the head of the family and for guests. His gourd water-pipe rested on the ground in front of him and he sucked slowly on its wooden tube. As he sat there smoking in silence, he seemed to be pondering whether Kerwagé would give birth to a second daughter, or to a son. Naturally, Bala hoped for a son.

Presently, as the cattle neared the house, Bala put down the tube of his pipe. He wrapped a little tobacco in a twist of the fiber of the false-banana plant, pouched it in his right cheek, and went outside to receive his cattle. One of his cows, the white one Gwad, if she was not welcomed with a swallow of tobacco juice would wander on into the darkness as if she had had nothing to eat all day. Her ear had been cut to break her of this habit of wandering, but it had not helped. She was already moving around the house toward the field of false-banana plants when Bala called her by name: Gwad! Gwad! She came back for her tobacco juice.

Four of the cattle entered the house, where Matebet led them to their places and tied them. The male servant Atshéwa led Bala's other cattle to his second house—for Bala was a man of wealth who owned not only two houses but also many head of cattle, only a few of which were pastured with the cattle of the village. Matebet prepared the clay tripod in the fireplace and put the iron kettle on to boil.

Bala wrapped himself in his blanket-toga, slipped off his trousers, and lay down in the *kakat.* His small daughter Theresa came up running and sat down beside him. Bala asked her to rub his back with her little hand. Theresa kissed his cheek. She slid the toga down slightly and started rubbing.

Kerwagé's labor began and she sighed heavily where she lay near the fire. At her daughter's birth, her labor had been severe and as a result she had used to say that she hoped God would never give her another child. But no one believed that she was sincere, for she did not yet have a son. Matebet, a woman of compassion, heard her mistress' heavy sighs and in pity laid a curse upon herself, crying: "O mistress, may I suffer in your stead!" For Matebet herself was a mother and knew what labor pains can be.

The coffee was ready now and Yibgyeta, a young man whose house was nearby, appeared for the evening gathering for the first time in over two weeks. He entered and greeted the household by saying: "How did you spend the day?" Bala raised his head and said to him:

"Is that you, Yibgyeta? Where have you been these days that we haven't seen you?" Without waiting for an answer, he went on: "Has your wife come back yet or does she still stay away from you?"

Yibgyeta, shy because of his youth, said, "she came back today."

"So, that's why you have come to our evening gathering . . . your wife has returned to you and can watch your house."

While the men conversed, Matebet prepared the coffee. She fetched the fiber base for the kettle and placed the kettle upon it. She washed the black ceramic cups and put them on a wooden tray. Atshéwa, the male servant, who had milked the cows in the other house

3

and given them salt-earth to lick, now joined the gathering. Kerwagé did not move from her place beside the fire and was silent except for occasional sighs. When she was asked if she would take coffee with milk, she refused. But little Theresa said: "There are more than enough cups. Why am I not given my coffee too?"

"Child," Matebet said brusquely, "do you expect to receive coffee before your elders have had their second cup?"

Bala, however, sipped a little from his cup and gave the rest to his daughter. "Here, take mine." Theresa was pleased and took the coffee with a smile.

When the coffee-drinking was over, Matebet, agitated by her mistress' pain and still crying to her in compassion, hastily put the tripod away, carried the coffee kettle into the *derar*, the storage part of the room separated from the rest by a wooden partition, and put away the cups, the tray, and the kettle-base. Kerwagé now asked that the women of the village be called to act as midwives, and Bala, sure that his wife was in labor, had the ground in the other house prepared with mats and straw so that he might rest there while Kerwagé gave birth. Atshéwa took his spear—for that day a cow had been killed in the neighborhood for a death commemoration, and the hyenas out in the fields could smell the blood and were dangerous. He went to call the women of the east side of the village, while Yibgyeta took his stick and went to call the women of the west side. The women of the village hurried to Kerwagé in their compassion for her, carrying torches of sticks and of broomsage because the night was now pitch black and because of the hyenas. When they arrived, Bala picked up his

4

small daughter, put on his wooden sandals, and went to his other house. Atshéwa and Yibgyeta went with him to keep him company through the night.

It was now midnight and everything was quiet. There was no sound of cattle or of goats or donkeys, not even the sound of a cock or a dog, nothing except the blowing wind and now and then the far-away howl of a hyena. One could also hear Kerwagé crying with pain from time to time. When she cried out, the women with her cried too: "O holy Mary, save us!" Bala grew worried but in order to conceal his disturbance, as a man should, he talked of other things. Now and then he caressed the cheek of his little daughter, asleep beside him, with the back of his hand.

The hyena made the waiting household very afraid that Kerwagé might die, for the superstition holds that if a hyena howls when someone is sick, then death is near. Atshéwa said: "O hyena, weep for yourself alone!"

"Amen," said Yibgyeta. "Let her weep for only herself."

Bala, being a Catholic, did not believe in such superstitions and told Atshéwa and Yibgyeta that they were talking nonsense. Deep in his heart, however, he was probably also afraid.

At cockcrow there was a new sound from the main house. Matebet, carrying her big knife on her shoulder from fear of the hyenas, came panting to Bala.

"Girl, what news do you bring!" cried Bala, afraid that something had happened to his wife.

"Master, my mistress has delivered a child!"

Bala breathed out his relief like a bellows.

"Is it a son or a daughter?"

5

"Master, I don't know what it is!" She ran back to the main house to ask. On her way, she tripped over a stone but scrambled up unaware that she had fallen. In a moment she returned, panting as before.

"Master, you have a son!"

For the second time Bala gave thanks to God.

Matebet was so excited that Atshéwa and Yibgyeta began to laugh at her and awakened Theresa. Bala picked his daughter up and went back to the other house. Everyone congratulated Kerwagé and then returned home to sleep.

During the morning many people came to congratulate her. Zemwet, too, an old friend of Kerwagé's, came from the village of Atat with her son Degemu, who was about six years old and already a student. She entered the house and went to where Kerwagé lay and kissed her, saying: "May I be split with pain in your stead!" Degemu also kissed Kerwagé, but silently.

Pleased with her friend's coming, Kerwagé with effort sat up and leaned against the wall. In a weak voice she said:

"Zemo, who told you that I had given birth? Or did the news travel to Atat by the wind?"

"My dear, I knew that you were due, and when I reached the village, I heard that you had delivered. The news has not yet gone so far as Atat."

"And so you have been out early in the cold morning as you should not be. If you don't think of yourself, you should think of your little son. The cold and dampness will kill him."

Kerwagé had not been outside and thought it was cold, but the sun was bright. The sky was clear. Morning dew fell from the grass in the fields, it penetrated the

7

house, and one could smell it. Inside the house, however, the room was partially dark. The door was just ajar so that the sun could not enter. It was feared that if the sun touched the woman-in-childbed and her baby, they would fall sick.

2

BALA GOES TO THE ASSEMBLY

The next day was the day appointed for the meeting of the Guragé tribal assembly at the *ajoka* in a certain village six hours' walk from Wardéna. The meeting was so important that no hero or elder could stay away, not even if there were a death in his clan. Bala, after ordering Atshéwa to buy honey for Kerwagé to eat after her childbirth, put the high-horned saddle on his black mule and departed.

All who held the title of hero or elder were present. Present were the hero of the Chaha, Kenyazmatch Amerga, or He Who Leads the Right Wing in War, and

9

the Gyeta hero Feetawrari, Vanguard in Battle; and Chief Bibi, and Azmatch Torena, He Who in Battle Is Always Near His Chief; and Gwetakweeya and the Damwa Neda; Wonzhetareb, the War Eagle, and Barkefete, He Who Breaks the Way for Others; all were there. The assembly was to concern itself with two matters, marriage laws, and the selection of the week when the Meskel festival would be celebrated. It was desired to arrange the date so that the Guragé festivities would coincide with those of other groups in various parts of Ethiopia.

The discussion began early in the afternoon when all the heroes and elders had gathered in the shade of the *ajoka zigba* tree, and salutations had passed. Kenyazmatch Amerga, seated in the middle of the assembly on a stool, began by pronouncing: "That our tongues may speak honestly. That the young may thrive. May the elders live long. May day become night without the happening of any evil. Long life to our emperor, Haile Selassie!"

As the assembly deliberated, people of the *ajoka*-village came with kettles of coffee and food for the elders and heroes; they came from right and left, from the four corners, from up and down, from all directions. At a little distance from the *zigba* tree grazed the lawmakers' mules and horses. On the other side, far enough away that their voices would not disturb the meeting, the children who had accompanied their fathers to lead their mules played in an open level pasture. From time to time Bala raised his head and looked toward the playing children and snapped his fly-switch. An old elder sitting beside him observed him, and nudged him with his elbow and said:

10

"What are you looking at so often? Is your son there?"

"No. I am thinking that the time will come when my son will play like that."

"How old is your son?"

"He was born at cockcrow this morning."

"May I congratulate you," said the old man. "Well, the children of today grow fast. You won't have to wait long."

The assembly ended about four and Bala bridled his mule and started home. He did not let the mule rest until he reached Wardéna, for the hour was late and he was worried about his wife. He arrived at home and Atshéwa took the mule into the stable of the other house to unsaddle it while Bala hurried into the main house. He sat on a stool in the *wofencha*, the front part of the room. Theresa ran to him, kissed his cheek, and took his hat and fly-switch and hung them on their wall-hooks. While Bala talked with Kerwagé about her day, Matebet brought the water bowl to wash his feet. Little Theresa stood at her father's knee and said:

"Father, have you seen the new baby?"

"Yes, my daughter."

"Will mother give birth to another baby today?"

He laughed and said: "Not today, my daughter."

That evening Yibgyeta and Atshéwa came to the evening gathering to ask about the meeting of the Gurage council. They laid their spears and sticks in the loft as Bala welcomed them, and they sat down in the *kakat*. Yibgyeta said:

"Elder, what was discussed today and what were the decisions?"

"After talking all afternoon we decided that the

12

Guragé shall celebrate Meskel at the same time as the Amhara, so there will be uniformity throughout Ethiopia, which, after all, is one country. Second, we ruled that from now on no bride-price shall be paid, more than the clothes bought for her."

Kerwagé overheard and said jokingly: "You have made such a law before Theresa is of an age to marry . . . and you report it as if you have ruled wisely?"

But Yibgyeta was pleased and said: "I'm going straight home and tell my wife. If she ever abandons me again, I won't let her come back. Now that girls are so cheap, I can marry any girl I want."

The discussion of the new marriage law ended only with the close of the evening gathering. The women grumbled about it among themselves, but the men were pleased.

3   KERWAGÉ AND ZEMWET

For two months Kerwagé and her new baby remained on their special bed behind the customary curtain of grass and jute. Bala fed his wife well so that she would regain her strength, and because she had given him a son and he wanted her milk to be rich. At no time did Kerwagé lack for meat or honey. She had been a beautiful woman before; now at the end of her seclusion she was twice as lovely. Her skin had lightened, too, for she had not been exposed to the sun.

The day Kerwagé left her bed and came from behind the curtain, her friend Zemwet came to congratulate her and visit. The bed and curtain had been removed when Zemwet arrived, and Kerwagé was in the *kakat* seated on a low stool, her son at her breast. Zemwet said: "O Kero, you have left the curtain looking well!"

"May your heart rejoice as mine does, Zemo! But you've come alone today. Why didn't you bring your little boy with you?"

"A week ago his father took him to Indibir."

"And why did he take the child to that land of drought and hunger?"

"He took him to the mission to go to school."

Kerwagé was astonished. "To the mission to school?"

"Of course, to school. What's so surprising about that?"

"You must be out of your mind, Zemo."

"Why?"

"And so you really sent him away to school! Shinega, my son, will never go to school, not even if my throat should be cut. Parents make their sons strangers by sending them to school. Kwerye's son finished his studies and lives in Addis Ababa and makes a lot of money, and he never comes home to see his parents, not even once a year . . . not even at Meskel! No, my son will never go to school, God forbid! God will give Shinega what he intends to give him, without any going to school. What difference does school make so long as a man has luck with him?"

"Pah! All I want is for Degemu to have a decent life. Let him study as long as he wants to, if it will help him. As for me, if God intended me to live alone, I can content myself."

While Kerwagé and her friend were talking, Bala came in from work sweating and with his head still covered by the large pumpkin-leaf he had tied on against the heat of the mid-afternoon sun. He had spent the whole day weeding the tall false-banana plants, until the gnats had begun to sting him and he became hungry. He took off the pumpkin-leaf and said hello to Zemwet. Matebet brought water for him to wash his hands. Kerwagé, interrupting her conversation, moved around the room preparing his meal. She broke a circular loaf of good *wusa*-bread into pieces and placed it on the low bamboo table. She set out a dish of cabbage, boiled and mixed with cheese and butter and seasoned with salt, red pepper, and other spices. While the adults ate, Theresa sat on a little stool beside her father and he fed her with his horn spoon.

When the meal was over and the table cleared, Kerwagé and Zemwet resumed their conversation. Bala left for a small neighboring village called Azer to look for Kartchea. Kartchea was a Fuga, the serving clan of those who worked in wood, who made pottery—especially the Fuga women—and who performed circumcisions.

Bala found Kartchea sitting in front of his house in the shade of a *wanshehena* tree making a wooden head-rest for sleeping. His black dog Gebtchuet lay near him, and in the shade of another *wanshehena* tree were three just-finished wooden stools wrapped in false-banana fiber to keep the green wood from warping and splitting. On the bare earth in front of the house, a fresh calf-hide was stretched to dry, and two vultures circled high above. To keep the vultures from coming down and spoiling the hide, Kartchea had thrust two spears upright in the earth. The black dog saw Bala first and

started barking. Kartchea put down his work and sprang to his feet. When he saw that it was Bala, a land-holding Chaha, he greeted him by saying, "Abiyet, master!"

"That on your hunt you may kill and eat, Kartchea!" Bala responded. "What are you carving today?"

"Master, I'm making a little wooden pillow to sell at market tomorrow."

They entered the house. The loft was filled with pottery, some of it black, some of it not yet fired. There were all sizes of water containers, large and small dishes, and different water glasses of clay, all made by Kartchea's wife, whose business was pottery. Bala could smell fresh meat hung below the loft behind the partition. He said:

"Have you Fugas been hunting? Where did you get all the meat?"

"No, master, we have not been hunting. The meat is a calf of Yibgyeta's. It died last night and he gave it to me."

"May God replace Yibgyeta's calf."

"Amen, master. And why have you come to see me today?"

"I've decided that it is time for my son to be circumcised. He is now two months old."

"When would you like me to perform the circumcision, master?"

"Five days from now, if that's convenient."

"No, I have other work to do five days from today. Will a week be too late?"

"Let it be a week from today."

So conversing, they walked out the front door and around to the rear of the house. The earth there was as bare as in front; there were no false-banana plants, no coffee trees, not even any cabbages. The dog followed them. A little distance away, thick smoke was rising from the bare ground. There his wife, Kartchea said, was firing some pots for market. Saying "We will meet next week," Bala departed.

4   SHINEGA'S CIRCUMCISION

On the appointed day Kartchea the Fuga arrived at Bala's house in the morning holding his small water-pipe in one hand, and in the other, his blacksmith-wrought razor. His black dog trotted behind. It was quite early and the village cowherds were just driving the cattle off to graze. But already a young bull had been slaughtered in front of the house, and skinned and the carcass hung inside; and butter had been melted, and beer of the fifth day set out, for the circumcision celebration. Vultures were on the bare earth pecking at coagulated puddles of blood where the bull had been killed. The black dog

20

stayed outside to share the vultures' meal while his master entered and greeted everyone with "Abiyet." The carcass of the bull had been hung on the other side of the central pillar and Atshéwa and Yibgyeta were cutting it up, half to be served at the circumcision, the other half to be sold for two Ethiopian dollars a piece of about three kilos. Bala was whetting the dull knives. Many small children squatted on their haunches watching with the hope of receiving bits of meat. Theresa had already been given a small piece from the hind quarter and was sitting near her father, chewing on it. Bala turned as Kartchea entered, put down his knife, and said loudly:

"Kartchea, may you kill and eat on your next hunt! How is it that you managed to remember your promise and come on time today?"

"Master, am I not always punctual when the work is for you?"

"That's true. You're a rare Fuga, Kartchea. You never say you'll do what you don't intend to, and if you say you're coming, you do come. Well, is it too early, or can the circumcision be done now?"

"I have another appointment in the afternoon, master, so I think we had better begin now."

Kerwagé, holding her baby in her arms, was staring at the razor. Her heart trembled. She said: "I will not sit here and look on while my son is cut." She passed the child to Bala, and left for the other house. Gentle Matebet wanted to leave too, but Bala told her to sit there and do her job.

Kartchea stropped the razor a last time. Bala held the baby's arms and Atshéwa held the legs apart. Deftly and quickly Kartchea performed the circumcision. In

21

the other house, Kerwagé heard her son scream, and she ran back crying: "May I have your pain, my little one, may I be given your pain!" Matebet began to moan. Theresa, frightened, huddled near Matebet.

Kartchea now washed his hands and accepted the portion of meat that was given him. Half he put aside for his wife at home; the rest he ate hurriedly.

"Why such haste, Kartchea?" said Bala. "Eat slowly, talk a bit, there's no rush."

"Sir, I have another appointment before two."

"Where?"

"At Atat, master."

"To split wood for someone?"

"Not to split wood, master. I must perform a throat operation on a child."

"Oh? So you'll feast twice today!"

"So long as there is a God of Chaha, there will always be feasts, sir."

Kartchea finished eating. The meat he had put aside he wrapped in a leaf of false-banana. He drank to the last drop the jar of beer he was given. Then putting a glowing coal in the bowl of his small water-pipe, and having taken two long puffs, he blessed the family, saying:

"May this be a home of joy and abundance! May the God of the Chaha let us live to see the wedding of your son Shinega!"

The Fuga Kartchea took his leave.

22

5 SHINEGA FALLS SICK

A circumcision wound sometimes leads to sickness, but Shinega's healed quickly and uneventfully. About six months later, the time for the false-banana harvest came. As was customary, Kerwagé hired some women of the village to work and asked others to help in exchange for the help she herself had given them at other times. First, Bala and Atshéwa stripped the leaves from the tall plants and spread them on the ground, and then they pulled up the trunks. The women took their stools into the grove and went to work. Some pounded the roots with toothed mallets. Others unpeeled the trunk's *gupa* layer by layer, and scraped the *gupa* to separate fiber from pith. Thus they prepared *wusa* to be baked into flat loaves of bread. As the women worked, they sang, one of them leading:

Wives of hard-workers, rejoice!
Your men planted hundreds of *essets!*
Luckless wife of a lazy man, what will you
give your crying children?
Wives of hard-workers, rejoice!
You have nothing to worry about.
Wife of a lazy man, dress and be up!
You must go to market and buy cheap!
Wives of hard-workers, rejoice!
        You are mothers to village orphans!
Wife of a lazy man, you have no rest!
        Both summer and winter you look for bread.

To each line, the women responded in chorus:

Oh, hard-working men, may no fire see your hands,
nor any evil!
Oh lazy men, find wisdom and spirit to labor!

While the women worked, little Theresa looked after Shinega in the house. She brought a false-banana flower and gave it to him to play with. It happened that a village weaver, a man named Abu, came to see Bala that afternoon on business. Bala was not there, for he had gone to the law-court at the Béro, about a forty-five-minute walk from Wardéna, where he liked to sit and listen to the trials. Abu asked Theresa where Bala was and she said she didn't know. "When he returns," said Abu, "tell him that I was here looking for him," and he

departed. Abu's head was large and bald and his body was thin, and from a distance he looked like a thin stick with a pumpkin stuck on top. Nor were his eyes like other men's; they were yellow.

No sooner had Abu left than Shinega started to cry. Theresa tried to quiet him and couldn't, so she went out behind the house among the false-banana plants and told her mother. Kerwagé, thinking the baby was hungry, hurried in to give him her breast. But Shinega refused to suck and went on crying. Kerwagé was very concerned; this had never happened before. Suspecting that Theresa might have pinched her brother when he became troublesome, Kerwagé asked her, but Theresa said no, she hadn't even touched him. So although Kerwagé was impatient to get back to her work, she had to stay for a while carrying the baby in her arms and singing him a lullaby until he went to sleep

The village women stopped work at dusk. Those who were poor took home some of the *wusa* they had made for the evening meal.

Shinega had waked when Kerwagé returned to the house, and was moaning and crying. By the time Bala came home, it was clear that the baby was sick. No one knew what had happened to him, unless perhaps Theresa.

Bala asked his wife, as usual, whether anyone had come to see him during the day. "No one," said Kerwagé. Then Theresa remembered Abu and told her father about him.

"What did you say?" Kerwagé asked in surprise. "Abu came today?"

"Yes, while you were working, he came to see father."

26

Kerwagé was alarmed now. "When Abu came, was Shinega naked or covered?"

"You didn't take time to dress him today when you went out to work. When Abu came, Shinega was naked playing with a flower."

"Oh, Lord! That's it! That's why the baby is sick! Once Abu looks on a cow, its milk turns to pus. If he looks on a child, that child is sure to die!"

"Pah, woman," said Bala to his excited wife. "Stop talking nonsense. Are you a Christian, that you still believe in the evil eye?"

Angrily Kerwagé retorted, "Christian or not, the evil eye remains the evil eye. The boy has never been sick before. So why should he get sick now? Oh, Lord, it's that evil eye of Abu's!"

The cure for the evil eye lies with the person who has the evil eye. Early the next morning, Kerwagé went and found Abu and took a pinch of earth from beneath his large foot. This she put in milk that she gave Shinega to drink. Bala, not knowing what his wife had done, saddled his black mule and set out to consult a Muslim sheik who was experienced in medicines. The sheik prescribed: "A horn-spoon full of *abasud* spice mixed with butter every morning until the child is cured, and the milk of a cow fresh for the first time."

For some six months Shinega was dosed with butter and *abasud* spice and milk. At the end of that time he was clearly well, but whether it was the medicine that had cured him, or the pinch of earth his mother had placed in his milk, no one could know for sure.

6   PLAYING RIDDLES

One spring day in Shinega's ninth year, late in the evening, Abu came for the evening gathering smoking a cigarette that he had made using a tender yellow leaf of corn-husk because he was out of paper. There was no one in the house except Shinega and Theresa. They sat by the fire keeping warm and playing riddles. Abu asked Theresa:

"Girl, where are your family?"

"Mother and Matebet are in the other house cooking supper. Father and Atshéwa have gone to look for the white cow Gwad."

"Slitting her ear did not break her of wandering off, did it?"

"She's been all right recently," said Shinega. "But tonight father and mother were so busy talking that he forgot to give Gwad her tobacco juice."

Abu laughed. "O boy, the habit of tobacco is not limited to humans these days. It passes even to cattle."

"She has always been that way."

Abu sat down and listened to the children's play as he waited for Bala and the others to return.

"Shinega, here is a riddle!"

"Say it!"

"Marks of a whip are on the body of an elephant."

"The rafters of an unthatched roof."

"Good! Here's another."

"Say it!"

"It eats when I eat, it walks when I walk, it sits when I sit."

"Your shadow."

"Right. Here is another for you."

"Say it!"

"We were two when we saw it, we were five when we picked it up, we were thirty when we ate it."

"I don't know."

"Give me cloth."

"Take the *kuta* cloth."

"May I gain riches, may I become important, through the *kuta* cloth. Two eyes saw it, five fingers picked it up, thirty teeth ate it."

"All right, now I have a riddle for you, Theresa."

"Say it!"

"It comes at night and it goes in the morning."

"Sleep."

"Here's another one, Theresa."

"Say it."

"It enters the forest making no noise."

"The sun?"

"No, you're wrong. Give me land."

"Take Gwebet."

"May I gain riches, may I become important, through the land Gwebet. The razor enters the forest of the beard making no noise."

"Here's a riddle for you," said Theresa.

"Say it!"

"On the back of the river, a drop of medicine."

"A bridge."

"Here's another."

"Say it."

"It's as sweet as the cabbage the girl cooked."

"Honey."

"You're wrong. Give me a mule."

"Take the gray mule."

"May I gain riches, may I become important, through the gray mule. An itch that is scratched is as sweet as the cabbage the girl cooked."

"Pah!" said Shinega. "All right, here is a riddle for you."

"Say it."

"I tie the sash of my father around my waist and there is no end to it."

"A path."

"All right, here's another riddle for you, Theresa."

"Say it."

"A beetle buzzes, a jar opens its mouth, the cedar tree falls."

30

"The buzzing beetle is mourning. The jar opens its mouth is the tomb. The cedar falls is the corpse."

Shinega and Theresa played riddles for a long time and Abu waited listening. But Bala did not return, not even in time for supper. The children stopped their game, and Abu went away.

This time he did not use his evil eye.

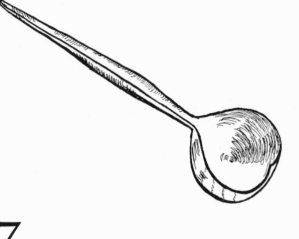

7

SHINEGA IS NAUGHTY

Until he was twelve, Shinega was mischievous and often rebellious. If he was told to do something he didn't want to, he would cry or pound with his fists. If he quarreled at play with Theresa, playing in the mud or sliding down a slippery clay hillside after a rain, he would pull her hair. When visitors came he had to be watched carefully or he would hide their walking sticks and flyswitches. When Kerwagé wanted to go to the market, he would cling to her skirt and hold her back. And sometimes when he felt he had not been given a large enough piece of cheese, he would throw the cheese on the ground angrily. In short, his chief occupation was making mischief.

When the boy reached his twelfth year, he began to tend his father's calves. Other village children his age were already going to school, but Shinega was not allowed to go to school. As Bala had many cows—not only those he kept in the village but also a large herd that stayed on the meadow grounds distant from Wardéna about six hours' walk—he thought that Shinega didn't need schooling; his son was wealthy already.

One day when Shinega and a playmate friend were near the village tending Bala's calves, they decided to steal ears of corn from a small neighboring farm, for the corn was nearly ripe. They left the calves munching grass and looked for a spot where the corn was tall and they wouldn't be seen. They chose ears of corn that had already been pecked open by birds. After they had eaten for some time, Shinega saw a caterpillar on the back of his friend's shirt, crawling toward his neck. "A caterpillar is on your back!" he cried. Frightened, the boy jumped out of the corn, tore his shirt off, threw the caterpillar down on the ground, and beat it with his stick. The insides of the caterpillar oozed out, and Shinega felt like vomiting. Now afraid to eat more corn, Shinega and his friend returned to where they had left the calves.

But the calves were not there. They looked right and left, but in vain. When they couldn't even find tracks, they decided the calves had probably gone back to the village because the afternoon sun was so hot. The boys went home empty-handed, but without a worry in the world.

Bala, sitting on his stool near the door twisting fiber into rope, saw Shinega approaching. He called to him: "Where are the calves?" Shinega knew that he was in trouble, but he tried to carry it off.

"When I went under the eucalyptus trees beside the river to look for a stick," he lied, "the calves wandered away."

Bala saw something white on his son's lips. Suspiciously he told him to come closer.

"What's that white stuff on your mouth?"

"This morning I didn't wipe my mouth after I drank my milk." Shinega looked at his toe twisting in the dust.

Bala now knew for sure that the boy was lying. He shouted at him:

"Why, you little liar! May you be broken into pieces and vanish! Those calves ran away while you were stealing someone's corn!" He jumped up and grabbed a stick to punish Shinega, but the boy fled around the house and across the plantation of false-banana, and hid among the coffee trees.

What had really happened was that the calves had wandered into a farmer's field of young corn, and the farmer had found them feeding there, and had taken them to his house. Bala had to go and pay for the damage the calves had done. Then he brought them home.

When darkness fell, Kerwagé was worried because Shinega had not come in and there were hyenas about. She went to look for him and found him crying in his hiding-place under a coffee tree. Shinega was in a dilemma: if he went home, his father would punish him, but if he stayed, the hyenas might attack him. Kerwagé reassured the boy: "May the village mourn my death if your father lays a hand on you!"

Shinega remained unconvinced, but when she told him the calves had been found, he felt better. Finally Kerwagé promised to buy him sugar tomorrow if he would go home.

8 SHINEGA ASKS FOR PANTS

The next day was Monday and Bala had some business to settle, so he left for the Béro early in the afternoon, after warning Shinega not to let the calves wander away again. The Béro was the place where marketing was done twice a week by the people of nearby villages. One also found the law-court there, a small school—the only one in a radius of about forty kilometers—and two modest restaurants and taverns.

About two hours after Bala left, Kerwagé and her daughter Theresa also started for the Béro. As they intended to buy barley, they drove the brown donkey along, so that on their return they would not have to carry the sacks themselves.

The path to the Béro twisted among the farms like a snake swimming a river. It was so narrow that two people could not walk abreast. The crowd of market-goers filled the path and spilled out on the grass to the sides and sometimes a little into the fields.

Kerwagé and Theresa had walked for about fifteen minutes when they were overtaken by Yibgyeta, who was sweating all over under the heavy sack he carried on his head.

"Courage, Yibgyeta!" Kerwagé greeted him cheerfully. "What are you selling today?"

"Lady, a few coffee beans."

"Why are you in such a hurry to sell coffee? Don't you know that you'll get a very poor price these days?"

"If I were to get no more than I would for mud, still I have to sell, for I've decided to go look for work in Addis Ababa."

"Don't you know that in Addis a man who has no job is taken away to Adola to dig for gold? Aren't you afraid that will happen to you?"

"Lady, I am alone in the world. It's a week today that my wife left me again and went back to her father. Only she and God know if she'll come back to me. I'm tired of working my fields alone. That's why I have decided to go to Addis."

"What are you going to do with your house, then?"

"All I can do is abandon it. If my wife changes her mind and comes back, she will live in it. If not, it will be empty until I return."

"Yibgyeta, it's poverty and loneliness that make

38

you wander away from us. But take my advice. You'll be better off to stay on the land of your fathers, even though it is not very comfortable, than to live in luxury among strangers."

They were still talking when they reached the Béro. Yibgyeta, still sweating heavily, went to the nearby river to wash his face. Children were playing there throwing stones in the water, and on the other bank, in the thick grove of eucalyptus trees, men must have been felling trees, for the sound of chopping could be heard easily. Kerwagé and Theresa accompanied Yibgyeta to the river and cooled their bare feet by wading up to their ankles. Then Yibgyeta headed toward the part of the market where coffee was bought, Kerwagé went to buy barley, and Theresa hurried off to the section where ladies' ornaments were sold. The butter with which Theresa had anointed her face attracted flies, and she brushed them away with a small leafy tree-branch she had picked up on the way.

The ladies' section was as crowded as the rest of the market. Theresa stopped in front of a boy who had spread his wares on a red and gray cloth on the ground. He had necklaces, rings, anklets, and bracelets, little bottles of perfumes, weaving yarns of all colors, earrings, hairpins, and pins and needles, spools of thread and buttons, anything and everything a girl could want. Theresa picked up a shiny ring and tried it on her little finger.

"How much?" she asked.

"Miss, that ring was made just for you. Look at it. I bought it at Addis Ababa for my sister, but as it is too small for her, I'm selling it. I should have taken her measure before I bought it, but I didn't think."

39

Suspecting that he intended to cheat her, she said: "I'm asking for the price, not a story."

"Miss, what do you want to pay for it?"

"What did you say? You're doing the selling! Tell me your price!"

"You mean my final price?"

"Yes, your final price."

"Miss, a dollar and a half."

"No, I'm not paying any dollar and a half for a tiny ring like that."

"Well, make me an offer."

"*You* tell *me*."

"Well, give me just a dollar and a quarter. Not a penny less."

"Will you take one dollar . . . or nothing?"

"No, Miss, that's impossible!"

Theresa slipped the ring off, returned it to him, and walked away. When she had moved a little distance, he called after her: "Miss, wait!"

"What!"

"If it were anyone else, I wouldn't do it. But I can see that you are the daughter of a man of wealth. I sell you the ring and maybe some day you may return the good turn. Give me your dollar and take it."

She paid the boy and went to find her mother. "I like the ring," said Kerwagé, "it's of good quality. But he cheated you by ten cents."

Kerwagé and Theresa spent the rest of the afternoon in the market making small purchases after long haggling, and at sunset they returned home, the donkey laden with the barley and other things they had bought. Shinega had already arrived with the calves. As for Bala,

40

he appeared last, for he had stayed at the Béro to drink potent anise-like *areki* and sweet honey-mead.

Theresa showed her brother her new ring.

"If they'll buy you a ring, why won't they buy me a pair of shorts? All the boys who are going to school now have shorts, but because I don't go, I don't have anything but a shirt."

Kerwagé, overhearing, said in agreement: "Yes, when your father comes home, ask him to buy you some shorts. Yibgyeta is going to Addis Ababa tomorrow. He can buy the shorts there and send them to you." Then she gave the boy the sugar cube she had promised to buy him and he skipped around the room with joy as he sucked it. Unfortunately, his mother suddenly saw a scratch on his knee and she said sharply: "Come here! How did you get that scratch?"

Shinega thought for a moment and then said: "I fell down while I was playing *zora*."

"You're lying. A cut like that isn't from falling down. Someone has scratched you with his fingernails. Who did you quarrel with today?"

"Am I supposed to stand still and look at him while he hits me?"

"Who?"

"Tourga."

"The boy who keeps calves with you? Haven't I told you not to quarrel with him? If you do it again, you won't be brought any more sugar."

"Do you expect me to stand there when he takes away my playing stick? I'll never do that, sugar or not."

The coffee was ready for the evening gathering. Bala arrived home and Yibgyeta joined them, leaving his empty house barred. Atshéwa did not come to the gathering, for he was tired; he had tended cattle all day and now was resting in the other house.

Bala had hardly sat down when Shinega ran to him and cried: "Father, will you buy me a pair of short pants?"

Bala stared at him.

"Who has spent the whole day advising you to ask me that? Or have you suddenly become a man?"

"All my friends have short pants. Do you want me to go around in only a shirt?"

Bala smiled.

"My son, we have more important things to think about than short pants. Wait until you are older."

Kerwagé, listening carefully, stepped in.

"It's just a little thing to buy the boy some shorts," she said to her husband. "Yibgyeta is going to Addis Ababa tomorrow. Give him some money, he can buy the shorts and send them back."

Bala ignored her. Looking at Yibgyeta, he said with surprise: "Are you going to Addis Ababa?"

"Yes. I've decided to leave tomorrow. I'll get a job and earn some money to pay my rent and taxes, with some left over for the Meskel celebration. Then I'll come back."

"Rent? Boy, haven't you heard about the land?"

"What land?"

"*Our* land. Dedjatch Bekfatu plans to sell it, and he has offered to let us buy it if we can."

Yibgyeta, of course, if he had no money for taxes or rent, could not think about buying land. So forgetting the matter, he left for Addis the next morning. He walked three hours to Wolkitte, which was on a road, and took a bus to the capital.

43

9 SHINEGA GOES TO WOLKITTE

Bala had refused to buy Shinega a pair of short pants and the boy knew that his father meant it. He was very disappointed and displeased, and about a year later spoke to his mother about the matter again.

"Mother, what do you think should be done about my getting some pants?" His voice was bitter.

"You know your father won't buy them. So what you had better do is go earn the money yourself. You're growing up now and you need money not only for a pair of pants but for other things, too."

"How can I earn money, with no money to start with?"

"There's coffee to be gleaned, if you exert yourself. A boy who really needs money can always find a way to get it."

"How can I glean coffee beans when I have to spend all the day tending calves? When will I find time?"

She was not convinced. "You really work so hard, don't you? Give up playing *zora* with the boys. Give up swimming. You'll have time enough to glean, then."

Shinega agreed and did as his mother suggested. For three months he gleaned coffee beans, and when he sold his gleanings, he found that he had made thirteen dollars. The pants he bought cost two dollars. With the rest of his money he started his little business as a trader: he bought soap at the Béro and sold it in the village. This he did for two years, but he found it not very profitable. With the money he had saved, he decided to go to Wolkitte and buy girls' merchandise wholesale, rings, perfume, necklaces, and so on, and sell retail in the Béro market. So one day he took the donkey, put his money in a little cloth bag that he hung around his neck, and went to Wolkitte. Before he had passed many villages he found himself traveling with other traders, but he did not know any of them. When they came to the ford, he watered his donkey.

To a village boy, Wolkitte was a large town. There was one not very wide asphalt-paved street with tin-roofed houses on either side. There were numerous small places of business, including tailor shops where the sewing was done by machine rather than hand. There were many bars and restaurants, and even hotels. The street was crowded with people, donkeys, mules, buses, and cars. The noise was ten times louder than the

Béro, and everyone seemed in a great hurry, rushing as if to a house of mourning.

Shinega tied his donkey to a tree and stood beside the street and stared at cars passing. The language around him was strange, Amharic instead of Guragé. As he stood there, someone came up behind him and grasped both his shoulders and asked: "Who are you?" Shinega was frightened, but when he turned, to his astonishment and relief he saw that it was Degemu, the son of his mother's old friend Zemwet, whom he had known all his life. His fright turned to joy.

Shinega had many questions to ask. "What do they call those things that run along the street like spiders?"

"Here they are called cars, but at home we know them as 'horses without tails.' "

"And that contraption that the boy is riding there?"

"At home it's known as 'Satan's horse,' but here it is called a bicycle."

"God, what wonders there are!"

Degemu chuckled.

"Is this where you go to school, Degemu?"

"No. I used to go in Indibir, but now I've finished and as soon as I have a suit made, I'm going to Addis Ababa to continue school there."

Shinega could not believe his ears. "But here you are already wrapped up like an ear of corn; pants, a shirt, a coat, and two shoes . . . you're wearing all this at the same time, and yet you want more clothes?"

Degemu, understanding the boy's innocence, smiled and said, "How is it that you've come to a place you don't know, with a donkey?"

"I'm going to trade in girls' merchandise and I came here to buy my stock."

47

"Do you know anyone here?"

"No, I don't."

"Can you speak Amharic?"

"I understand what people say, but I can't reply to them."

Degemu told him that the merchants in Wolkitte would be sure to cheat him, so fresh from a village. Therefore he took Shinega to introduce him to a Guragé friend who could be trusted. Then he said goodbye and went about his own affairs.

Shinega made his purchases, loaded the donkey, and started for home. As it was already late, he could not reach Wardéna that same day, and he had to ask hospitality, which of course was given as custom required in a land where inns are so far apart, at a farm beside the path.

That night Kerwagé was very worried when her son did not return. Bala grew angry and scolded her "It's all your own doing. You send the boy away into trade instead of keeping him in his warm home. Wild boys in Wolkitte may have seen that he is from the country, and maybe they have stolen his money, or maybe the donkey was frightened by the noise there, and bolted away. Or maybe the boy just got lost."

"Ah! You're the cause of it all! Have you forgotten that when he asked you to buy him a small pair of short pants, you told him that you had something more important to think about? Were you afraid that if you bought him the pants, you wouldn't have money enough left to buy land from the *dedjatch?*"

"A woman can understand only petty affairs! Why didn't you buy him the pants yourself? Why did you force him to go into trade?"

"Doesn't the boy have a father? Since when is the mother expected to buy her family clothes? Is he an orphan? As if it weren't enough for me to have to buy cheese and butter!"

"As if there were not a single cow in the house!"

"Should one be so impressed by the two cups of milk we get from the two cows you provide? Is that sufficient to feed a family and provide hospitality to guests?"

"Woman, enough now! Stop it!"

Bala and his wife spent most of the night in recriminations that did not ease their worry about Shinega. But late the next morning, the boy and his donkey arrived safe and sound. Theresa saw him first, in the distance, and ran to welcome him, crying: "May I stand from lying in mud!" Matebet also ran out, and helped Shinega unload the donkey. Shinega entered the house and his mother shouted: "May I rise from death! So, you're back safe!"

"I'm fine," the boy said as he sat on a stool to rest.

Kerwagé ordered Matebet to make a fire and put the iron griddle-pan on. She herself ran out behind the house and got fresh cabbage from the garden. Kerwagé cooked the cabbage on the griddle, then minced it and mixed it with butter and cheese, and gave it to her son thinking that he must be very hungry.

"Last night your father and I argued a long time. We were very worried about you."

"I didn't go to a battle. Why were you so worried?"

"My son, you don't know yet what it is to be a parent. One day, when you marry and have a son of your own, you'll understand."

10 SHINEGA GOES TO ADDIS ABABA

After three years in business for himself, Shinega had made about as much money as he could expect to, though at that not much. As he went to Wolkitte often and had made friends there, he had heard a lot about Addis Ababa, and his great desire was to visit Addis when he had saved money enough. When he was sixteen, he heard one day that corn was selling very high in the capital, and he said to his mother: "They say that corn is high in Addis Ababa now. Here in the Béro one can buy four ears for ten cents, but in Addis, only two. What do you say to my taking a couple of donkey loads to Addis to sell? I'll make a good profit."

"My son, if you go to Addis Ababa you will certainly make a profit. But what I am afraid of is that in your youth you may be tempted to stay there. Addis is like a sea, and everyone who goes there is swallowed up. Yibgyeta said that he would be back for Meskel, and now it's four years and we haven't seen him yet. Degemu, Zemwet's son, has written only two letters in the three years he has been away. If you go and stay as they have, that's bad."

"I swear upon the breast that suckled me, Mother, that I will come back. Let me take two donkey loads of corn to sell in Addis. With the money I make, I'll buy things to bring back and sell in the Béro. That way I'll have a double profit."

One day soon after this discussion, Shinega loaded two donkeys with corn and went early in the morning to Wolkitte accompanied by Matebet, who was to drive the donkeys home. They unloaded and Matebet left with the donkeys, but Shinega had to wait until evening and take the truck to Addis because he had missed the morning bus. As the driver had the habit of stopping often to drink honey-mead, and as he drove slowly between stops, the truck did not reach the capital until the next morning.

Shinega had imagined that Addis Ababa would be like Wolkitte. When he saw Addis' hurrying people, he thought they must *really* be insane. Vendors crowded the bus station, where the truck unloaded. Some of them leaned against walking sticks and had big baskets on their heads and were shouting: "Who wants bread? Who wants bread?" Others with boxes slung from their necks cried: "Who wants razors, soap, safety pins?" Others had mirrors and combs. Meanwhile a throng of

porters were pushing to get to the luggage first. Two of them got into a fight about a box and in an instant both were bleeding from the nose. Shinega was frightened by the noise and confusion and just stood motionless staring. A thief could easily have walked off with his bags of corn, and the boy would never have noticed.

Fortunately, however, on that morning it happened that Yibgyeta had come to the bus station to see off a friend returning to the country, and he spotted Shinega from a distance and recognized him. He ran up and cried:

"Aren't you Shinega?"

"And you, aren't you Yibgyeta?"

They kissed cheeks and Yibgyeta said:

"You've grown, boy! Are you well?"

"Fine! And how are you?"

"Well, well. And how are the people of Wardéna? Your father and mother, Atshéwa, all the rest?"

"Everyone is fine."

"Anyone sick? Have there been any deaths?"

"No one is sick and no one has died."

"Why have you come to this city that is strange to you?"

"I heard so much about Addis that I decided to see it myself."

Yibgyeta suddenly laughed. "So now you are wearing those pants you asked your father for the night before I left!"

"Yes, but he never bought them for me. I earned the money myself. Thanks to my mother, I went into the trading business."

"So how is the village?"

"Just as you left it. Nothing has changed."

"You must be joking. I see that you have changed!"

"But nothing else."

"How about your sister, is she married yet?"

"Not yet, though many fathers have come to ask her hand for their sons. Every day more come. Father wanted to give her to the son of a man from Gyeta, but Mother refused."

"Refused? Why? Isn't the family a good one?"

"That wasn't it. Though Theresa is a grown woman, Mother says she is still too young to marry."

"Well, it's not uncommon for mothers to want to hang on to their daughters. *Gari, gari!*" Yibgyeta called. Two passing carts wheeled in quickly and stopped, and their drivers got out and helped load Shinega's corn. Shinega and his friend got in one *gari*, the other followed with the corn, and they trotted off for Yibgyeta's dwelling-place.

All of Addis Ababa seemed in a hurry, and Shinega couldn't understand why. There were large cars and small cars and trucks and carts and motorcycles and bicycles, all whirling like devils and making devil-like noises. Men hurried along the sidewalks with bundles of firewood or wide high baskets of cabbages on their heads. And almost everyone wore shoes, even Yibgyeta, and the shoeshine boys on corners polished as fast as spiders. "They must all be out of their heads!" Shinega thought to himself. Aloud he said:

"I believed that Addis Ababa would be like Wol-kitte. I thought there would be just one long street. How can people find their way around? All the streets look the same and they go in all directions. And all the houses are the same, too. If I hadn't met you today, I could have been kidnapped!"

54

"That's true, Shinega. When I saw Addis for the first time, I felt like someone going into a dark jungle at midnight. But by and by one gets used to anything. Now I know the city as well as I know my own house."

They arrived at Yibgyeta's house and carried the corn in. Yibgyeta went to a shop to buy bread. Then he made tea and they ate breakfast together. Yibgyeta could stay no longer, for he was a waiter in a restaurant in a hotel and had to go to work. Shinega, tired after the night on the truck, lay down on his friend's bed, the first time he had ever slept on a mattress.

In the evening Yibgyeta returned and found the boy sitting on the edge of the bed thinking. "What are you thinking about, Shinega?" he asked.

Shinega smiled ruefully. "I was wondering if the people of Addis Ababa ever urinate. I went outside to look for a field, but there was nothing but streets and the streets were as full of people as this morning. So I had to come back."

Yibgyeta laughed. "The people in Addis don't urinate in the fields like at home. They have special places. Come along, I'll show you. It's on our way to the restaurant."

They left the house. The moon was shining that night, but electric lights twinkled everywhere like stars so that one could hardly tell it was moonlight. At the public urinal many men were standing in line waiting their turn and the smell was strong. Yibgyeta and Shinega waited until their turn came, and urinated. Then they went to the restaurant.

A piece of white cloth with a red cross hung at the entrance to the restaurant. Inside were five men dipping bread into peppery-smelling meat-stew. There were no more than ten small tables, bare of top with simple straight wooden chairs. Shinega and his friend ordered bread and stew and resumed their conversation.

"Shinega, how did the business of the land turn out?"

"What do you mean?"

"When I left, the *dedjatch* was about to offer it for sale."

"Well, every year they say it's finally going to be settled, but we have to pay taxes and rent as usual. Half the price of the land has already been paid. Only you and two very poor families haven't paid anything at all. In addition, we gave the *dedjatch's* agent a thousand dollars as a bribe. But Dedjatch Bekfatu told us that he won't sell his land by pieces . . . everyone must pay and the whole section bought at once."

"In that case it won't be settled for many years, for there are those who can't pay their share. As for me, I won't pay a cent. Anyone who wants to can buy my little farm."

"Yibgyeta! How can one part with the land of his fathers?"

"My father rented the land just as I did. Who really owned it? What do we mean when we say our 'fathers'' land? There's no such thing as land today, today everything is cash . . . and the place to get cash is here in Addis. From now on I'm forgetting the land. I'm going to stay here."

"You say that because you've lived here so long. By the way, if I may change the subject, do you ever see Degemu? When his mother Zemwet comes to visit, he is all she can talk about. She worries about him all the time because she never hears from him."

"I see him every Sunday. He is free Sundays, and he gets permission from the authorities of his school and comes to the hotel where I work and takes tea there. You can meet him there tomorrow."

The next day in the afternoon Shinega and Yibgyeta went to the Hotel Arennet. The restaurant in the hotel was not a small one like the place where they had eaten the night before. A few late lunchers were there. Opposite the door was a bar with shelves lined with every possible liquor. To the right of the door, a small table radio was playing. Shinega had never been inside such a fine building and he suddenly felt as frightened as a tiny boy lost among strangers. Yibgyeta told him to take a chair, and went to the kitchen to change into his waiter's uniform. He returned with tea.

Degemu came into the restaurant. It was easy to tell that Shinega was from the country, not only because of his clothes but also because he was listening with open mouth to the radio, quite forgetting his fear. Shinega's face was familiar to Degemu, but he could not quite place him. Yibgyeta, watching both boys, believed that they did not recognize each other. He came to Shinega and said: "Don't you know him?"

Degemu suddenly cried out: "Isn't this Shinega?"

"Yes, grown up now."

Degemu rose and, shaking hands after the manner of the capital, said: "Shinega, when did you arrive?"

"Only yesterday."

"It's surprising how people can change so quickly. Wasn't it at Wolkitte that we last saw each other?"

"Yes, the day you came up behind me and scared me."

Degemu remembered Shinega's remark that he was

"wrapped up like an ear of corn" that day, and smiled a little.

"Would you recognize me if you saw me in the street?"

"Of course I would! I knew it was you the minute you walked in the room."

"Why didn't you say hello then?"

"Because when you said nothing, I was afraid you preferred not to speak with me. Are you still going to school, or are you working now?"

"School, school . . . still! Studies never end. Yibgyeta, may I have some tea, too?"

"You aren't fat like Yibgyeta. Don't they feed you well at school?"

"Oh, there's plenty of food. Milk is as plentiful as water. They don't make coffee in a small kettle as we do at home. They make it in a barrel and it flows from a tap like water."

"In that case, you must be studying too hard to get fat . . . or maybe you worry too much."

The innocence of the boy's words made Degemu smile again.

"How's my mother?" he asked. "Do you ever see her?"

"She's fine, except that she worries because she never has news about you. Meskel is very soon now. Why don't you come home and see your parents for four or five days?"

"Why go home for Meskel? It's celebrated here too."

"Well, the main thing is not Meskel but to see your mother. Have you forgotten her already?"

"No, I haven't forgotten anyone. But village life

doesn't quite appeal to me now! To sleep on straw instead of in an iron bed! No radio and no newspaper . . . one just sits and listens to the nonsense and stories of the old folks. There isn't even a bar one can visit when one feels like it. On top of everything, there's no electricity and the smoke from the fire stings your eyes. No, thank you, it's too boring to think of going back to all that."

Shinega listened carefully and said to himself: "What mother says so often is true: education makes people strangers."

After a little silence, Degemu asked: "What brings you to Addis? Are you looking for work?"

"No, I had a better reason. I brought some corn to sell. After I sell it tomorrow, I'm going back home."

"Then I hope you'll tell my mother that you have seen me and I am well. I won't be able to see you tomorrow or the day after, for I have classes Mondays and Tuesdays."

Degemu finished his tea. He put ten cents on the table, and said goodbye.

Shinega stayed in the restaurant all afternoon listening to the music from the radio. In the evening he went home with Yibgyeta. The next day, he sold his corn, as he had planned, bought his merchandise, and took the bus back to Wolkitte.

11   ZEMWET PAYS A VISIT DURING MESKEL

On the third day of Meskel, the day called *nik-bar*, Zemwet came to visit Kerwagé for two reasons: first, to give her the customary holiday greetings, and second, to learn whether Shinega had brought any news of Degemu back from Addis Ababa. It was the end of the rainy season and the sky seemed to shimmer; there was not one speck of cloud. The wild flowers blossoming in clusters beside the path looked as though they were showing their teeth in laughter. The grassless yard in front of Bala's house had been scraped and made neat for Meskel, and the flat gray stepping stones had been scrubbed.

When Zemwet entered Bala was seated as usual on a mat in the *kakat* smoking his big water-pipe. Shinega was stretched out on another mat just in front of the storage section of the room. Theresa and her mother sat near the fireplace talking. The doormat was new and had been bought especially for the holidays. The Meskel meat could be seen through the partition and the loft was piled high with damp white firewood. The walls had been freshly whitewashed, and the black jugs and bowls and platters hanging in a row on the wall were shiny, some of them new and others newly polished.

"I am happy that you are in good health to see this Meskel," said Zemwet, the customary holidays greeting. She kissed Bala on both shoulders and the forehead and kissed Kerwagé on both shoulders. Kerwagé rose and responded:

"May we again have a good year!" She kissed Zemwet's shoulders. Then Theresa took the little bowl of butter Zemwet had brought as a Meskel gift, and put it behind the partition on the floor beneath the hanging meat. She returned and kissed Zemwet's cheeks, and Shinega got up and kissed her cheeks, too. Theresa poured beer into a clay glass and presented it to the guest. Zemwet took two swallows and pronounced judiciously: "Even if it weren't Meskel, I would have come only for this beer!"

Kerwagé smiled, pleased that her beer was appreciated. "Zemo, how is Meskel in Atat this year?"

"For some, abundant; for others, scant. Some have killed fat bulls, others thin ones. My husband slaughtered a delicious young bull and sold none of the meat. But what kind of Meskel can it be for me when my son is not at home? Every Meskel I spend as if I were bar-

ren. When I think of Degemu while I am feasting, the food does me no good, it simply disappears."

In a scolding tone Kerwagé said: "What I dislike most is for one to regret what she did willingly and knowingly. Didn't you yourself send your son away to school? Who forced you? So, why do you talk so foolishly now, as if you had done it against your will?"

"You don't understand, Kero. It's true that I sent him to school willingly, but I never thought that he wouldn't come back to see me, at least during Meskel. I never thought he would love me less simply because he studied and learned and knew more. Well . . . I wish him only good luck and I pray God no bad news of him ever reaches me." She wiped her tears with the back of her hand.

Shinega, listening, said: "I saw Degemu in Addis Ababa. He is just fine, and he sent his greetings to you through me. When I asked him about coming home for Meskel, he told me that he can't come because he has too much to do at school."

"My son!" Zemwet cried. "When will he finish studying, did he tell you?"

"If we are to believe his words, he will not finish before he is an old man."

"How can that be? Boys who had studied no longer than he are already working and earning more than three hundred dollars a month. What can he possibly have in mind keeping on so long?"

Kerwagé could not believe her ears. "Did you say three *hundred* dollars a month, Zemo?"

"Yes, my dear, three hundred."

"Three hundred dollars in a single month! If we could count all the money we have earned all our lives, it wouldn't be that much! And he goes on studying to earn more, as if that isn't enough? Is no one satisfied with what is clearly wealth? God, you are almighty!"

Zemwet felt much better now that she had heard the news about Degemu. Probably she would have continued to talk about him indefinitely if her attention had not been distracted by Theresa, who came to refill her glass with beer. She noticed that the girl's round breasts stretched her sleeveless cotton sweater tight.

"Kero," she said, "does no one come to ask for this girl?"

"Many come, but I refuse them all."

"But why? Aren't the families honorable, or the sons worthy?"

"I won't talk about it. No matter who comes, rich or of family, I will not give up my daughter this year. God forgive me that I should give away a daughter born only yesterday!"

Theresa, embarrassed at the turn the conversation had taken, walked out to go to the other house. Zemwet continued:

"Have you forgotten the saying that a calf born at home becomes a cow unnoticed? Since when are girls forced to become old maids with sagging breasts before they are given to a man?"

"Zemo, even *you* talk like that! Even *you* see Theresa with the eyes of a stranger!"

"I say it only for the girl's own good. If she hasn't finished growing yet, she'll certainly finish after she is married."

Bala smoked silently. Shinega rose and stretched his arms and went outside. He saw that the heat of the sun had lessened with the coming on of evening. He ran back into the house as if he had forgotten something, and Zemwet asked him what time it was.

"The sun is low, it's about four," said the boy. He went out to play carrying the inflated bladder of the bull that had been killed for Meskel.

"I've stayed too long!" said Zemwet. "I meant to stay only long enough to have a cup of coffee."

"You're always in a hurry," said Kerwagé. "You no sooner come than you leave. You don't even allow a conversation to be finished. Today is Meskel and there is nothing to hurry you. I'll make supper soon. Then we'll eat and talk as much as we want. And *then* you can go."

"No, my dear. If I stay any longer my husband won't let me back in. I left him alone in the house, and if someone should come calling, who will be there to offer the beer?"

"In that case, you are right to go. At the end of Meskel week I'll come and see you on a market day. I'll come early before going to the market."

Zemwet stood and took her leave.

12 BALA REPLIES TO A SPEECH

After Meskel the people of the Chaha tribe, well rested and feeling healthy and strong, resumed their usual work. Those who had bought their Meskel meat on credit now began to settle up, some with cash, others paying with labor. A few days later Dedjatch Bekfatu came in person from Addis Ababa in order to make an end, once and for all, to the business of the sale of his land. The important men from the villages around the Béro went to welcome him with gifts. Some took him chopped raw meat made tastier with butter and salt and pepper. Others offered beer and honey-mead in jugs. Bala, as the rich owner of a hundred head of cattle, came with a young bull. Shinega accompanied his father.

When they arrived at the Béro, Dedjatch Bekfatu was seated among the country people discussing crops and the weather. He sat there in the dress of a man of Addis, a black coat and a tall black hat. He was dark of complexion, almost black, and on his forehead was the long pale scar of a wound he had received during the last war. Seated, he did not appear a tall man.

Shinega observed the *dedjatch* fixedly for some minutes and then softly asked his father:

"Can this man be with child?"

Bala laughed silently but whispered back, "Don't say such things about a *dedjatch*."

Shinega persisted. "Then what makes him so fat?"

A little afraid that they were overheard, Bala said: "The *dedjatch* does not have to sweat the way we do. He doesn't have to jerk a plow or swing a sickle. He never has to walk far. That's why he is fat. Now don't ask any more questions. Just listen, like a boy should."

Dedjatch Bekfatu was indeed so fat that ordinary stools were not large enough for him, so he had been given a special one. He sat on it looking like a large vulture squatting on a fence-rail balancing with its wings somewhat spread. When he spoke, his breath came short and heavy like the breath of a runner. It seemed that the rolls of fat around his neck almost choked him.

The afternoon was spent discussing the sale of the land. Those who, like Bala, had money enough paid their full shares of the purchase price. But there were many, like Yibgyeta, who had nothing to pay with. Dedjatch Bekfatu made an angry speech, and so that everyone could understand, an interpreter translated from Amharic to Guragé:

67

"There are many men of wealth who would happily pay me cash for the land on which you live. Dedjatch Gerrefu, for example, or Grazmatch Djibu or Kenyaz-match Netteku. If I should offer the land to one of these men, I would receive cash in full the same day. But for your own good, I wanted to sell *you* the acres that have been cultivated so long by your fathers. That was why I asked you to bring your money today. Indeed, I even extended the day by two weeks! But many of you have come without the payment you promised. Now I can no longer wait! Don't blame me if I sell your land else-where. It will be your own fault."

Everyone was apparently impressed by the *ded-jatch's* speech. He was so kind to them! Bala stood, ad-justed his toga appropriately, and gave a few words of thanks:

"We have always been happy living on your land. No one has ever been imprisoned for failure to pay his tax and rent on time. No one who was delinquent in paying has ever had to give up a cow as surety. Really, what difference does it make whether you own the land, or we own it? Nevertheless, we are pleased that once you decided to sell, you offered it first to us who live upon it. No one could be more generous!"

Concluding these dry remarks with an ironical bow, Bala sat in his place again. The meeting soon ended and the men of the villages dispersed. Bala stayed behind a few minutes to present the *dedjatch* with the young bull, and then he and Shinega walked home.

Bekfatu spent the night at the Béro feasting on the bull. The next morning he left for Addis, taking with him what money he had collected.

68

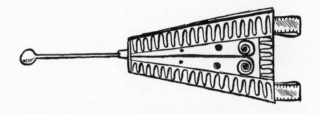

13   KERWAGÉ VISITS ZEMWET

As Bala had only one son, he wanted Shinega to marry soon. At sixteen and a half the boy was already tall. For four years he had conducted his own business, earned his own money, and bought his own clothes. He had traveled farther than Bala himself had ever traveled. He had learned to speak Amharic, which Bala only understood. So the boy was in many ways a man, but so long as Theresa, his older sister, remained a maiden, he could not marry because of what people would say. Therefore Bala decided to take the matter up with his wife.

"Kero, what have you decided about Theresa?"

"I won't give her up this year, not even if the dead rise from their graves."

"Well, in my opinion we should give her to the son of the man from Gyeta. He is of an important family, the grandson of the warrior Wonzhetareb Namaga. The boy is handsomer and stronger than the others who have been proposed. His father has wealth, so that our daughter will want for nothing. What more can you ask?"

"Even if he were the son instead of merely the grandson of the Wonzhetareb, I would not give her up. Not even to the son of a king!"

"Well, then, listen to me."

"What?"

"Let us betroth her to the grandson of Wonzhetareb Namaga, but let the wedding be delayed until Meskel two years from now. Meanwhile, I'll look for a bride for Shinega. They can both marry at the same time."

Though Kerwagé was stubborn about Theresa, the thought that her son would marry pleased her. When she had prevented him from going to school, it had been with the intention—among other things—that he should marry young. Therefore she agreed.

A few days later Kerwagé walked to the village Atat, accompanied by Theresa, to see her friend Zemwet. Zemwet welcomed them by crying:

"Kero, may I get up from lying in mud!"

"I too, Zemo.

"But you said you were coming right after Meskel. Now it's six months and over. I was about to go to Wardéna myself, thinking something must be wrong."

"My dear, one has so much to do! The floor to be swept, clothes to be taken to the river, coffee for visitors, cooking, manure to spread under the coffee trees. How could I slip away? But so long as I have my health, thank God, it's all right!"

Zemwet asked for Kerwagé's news and Theresa, embarrassed before a word was said, left to visit a girl-friend in the neighborhood.

"Zemo, I have brought great news!"

"And what is it?"

"I've betrothed my daughter to the grandson of the Wonzhetareb of Gyeta."

"What! You make yourself so stubborn for so long, and then give in at the end? Well, I always knew you would, sooner or later. When will the wedding be?"

"Not the Meskel to come but the one after. But that isn't all! My husband is busy looking for a bride for Shinega. Just yesterday Bala ordered the Fuga Kartchea to start making boards for a new house. Our son will be married at the same time his sister is."

"You are certainly joking!"

"I swear it! If it isn't true, may I die!"

"What a pity. Is it possible that yesterday's child is to marry already?"

"Zemo, nowadays one judges by a boy's growth, not his years. There is no reason for us to be ashamed in marrying him young. And you, what have you heard about Degemu recently?"

"Someone who saw him said that he is all right and has grown to be a man. He himself wrote me a letter not long ago."

"Is he coming home?"

71

"You speak of his coming home! If only he would stay in Addis Ababa, that would be as good as his coming home."

"Kero, what do you mean?"

"He wrote that he intends to go beyond the sea when he finishes his studies at Addis Ababa. Only God knows why he has made such a decision. Well, well . . . I've always let him have his own way. I only hope God will let me live to see him married, in spite of everything. All his friends have taken wives, some of them have children. I wait with hope, but . . ."

Kerwagé smiled drily.

"You think that a son who has not returned to his village for a single Meskel in over six years will come back to take a village bride?"

"If he marries anywhere else, he will no longer be my son!"

"My dear friend, you had better resign yourself. Educated young men never marry our daughters. They prefer girls who like themselves have been to school, no matter what sort of girls they may be otherwise. Didn't the son of Kwerye marry a mulatto in Addis? And did he even invite his own parents to such a wedding? And what could they do, except curse him and try to forget him?"

"Ehhh!" Zemwet nodded morosely.

Theresa returned. Zemwet dried her tears and got up to prepare food.

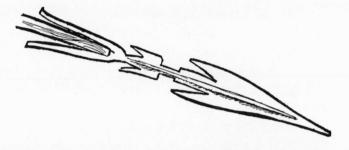

14 THERESA GETS SICK

Shinega did not know that his father was looking for a bride for him, but when Bala ordered lumber prepared for a new house, the boy began to suspect what was afoot. One day when he came into the eucalyptus grove to urinate, he saw Atshéwa off at a distance chopping firewood for the evening meal, and he went to talk with him. Atshéwa grinned and said:

"Shinega, I suppose you are pleased that your father has found such a beautiful girl for you."

The boy pretended not to understand.

"But she looks pretty well-developed to me,"

73

Atshéwa went on, watching him. "Are you sure you can handle her?"

Shinega felt ill at ease. He was a little confused: on the one hand, he thought that Atshéwa might be joking; on the other hand, for after all, a new house was going to be built, it might be true.

Atshéwa put his ax down and leaned it against a tree. He wiped his sweat and sat on a log to rest.

"You mean you really don't know that you're engaged now?"

"No one has said anything to me."

"You've been engaged for one week today. Your bride often comes to the Béro market. I think she sells bamboo basket-tables there. If you want to see her, we'll go to market together some day and I'll show her to you."

"When will my marriage be?"

"Meskel after next, at the same time your sister is married."

Shinega was excited and elated. He felt that he had become a man. At the same time, he was somewhat worried, for he didn't know what a man does when he marries.

Atshéwa rose, picked up his ax, and resumed chopping. Shinega walked home silent with thought. When he arrived, he found the lower half of the door closed, for a little wind was blowing and Theresa, who was not feeling well, was lying down.

"What's happened to her?" Shinega asked.

"She has a headache."

"When did it start?"

"A long time ago, the day we went to visit Zemwet.

The sun was too hot and it made her head hurt. But the pain didn't become bad until today."

"Why don't you put cold butter on her head, then?"

Kerwagé nodded. She laid the fly-switch on the mat and went behind the partition into the *derar* and got two horn-spoons of cool butter. She put the butter on Theresa's head and to keep it from ruining her clothes when it melted, covered it with a leaf of the false-banana tied with a strip of muslin. The coolness of the butter made Theresa feel better. Her breathing deepened, and soon she went to sleep.

She did not lose her headaches, however. Time passed, and every day she had to spend several hours lying down.

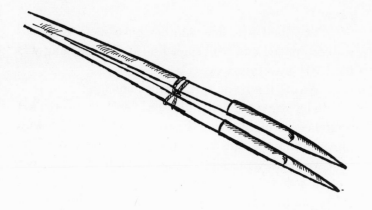

15 DEGEMU TELLS ABOUT LIFE AT INDIBIR

Degemu finished his studies at Addis Ababa, and when the time came for him to go beyond the sea, he returned to Atat to take leave of his parents. The next day Shinega went to see his friend very early. When he arrived, Degemu had just gotten up and was sitting in the sun in the entrance to the house wearing his Addis Ababa clothes. They shook hands in the Addis manner.

"Degemu, we didn't expect you," said Shinega. "From what you told me in Addis, I thought you would never come home again. If you had let me know that you were coming, I could have met you at Wolkitte with a mule."

"I myself didn't think I would come. But suddenly I felt guilty about going abroad without seeing my parents to say goodbye."

"Good. How did you spend the night? Didn't you feel a stranger eating village food and sleeping on straw?"

"The food was fine. Mother gave me a delicious dish of minced and well-spiced meat. But sleeping was hard. My eyes didn't close."

"Wasn't the straw spread thick enough?"

"The straw was all right, but the bugs weren't. I scratched all night. Even the soles of my feet itch with bites. I think the fleas have crawled under my skin."

"Well, they probably found you a feast, with your feet so soft from wearing shoes." Shinega removed a safety pin from his shirt and knelt and with the point of the pin pricked two fleas loose from the sole of Degemu's right foot. "Maybe you're sorry you came home."

"Not at all. I'm rather glad I came. If I hadn't, I would probably have forgotten completely what village life is. And the village reminds me of my years at Indibir."

"You never told me about Indibir, except to say that you went to school there. What was it like?"

Zemwet had toasted bread, mixed cabbage with cheese and butter, and milk. She called the boys to come in to breakfast.

"If I try to tell you everything, there'll be no end. But I'll tell you a few of the things that stand out.

"My first day there was a Sunday. Father took me. The boys had permission to leave the mission for the afternoon, so everything was quiet. My father presented me to the head priest, and then left.

78

"I felt like crying. I ran after father, but he mounted his mule and rode away. I wanted to call him back, but I was crying so hard I couldn't. At that time I was very small and I just stood there and wept as father disappeared. I was afraid. Of course, there was really no reason to be afraid. I thought I would never see my parents again, and I decided I would feel better if I went into the mission church and prayed. I prayed for some time, kneeling and no longer crying, and when I left the church, the boys had returned to the mission. One of them, his name was Welde Senbet, saw that I was new and came to talk with me. While we were talking the bell rang and he told me it was for supper. Before our fried wheat was given to us, we prayed. The boys took their tin plates and ran to be served. Those who were behind began to shout, 'I didn't get any, I didn't get any!' As for me, I had no plate. Welde Senbet saw that I had nothing and told the boys to be quiet a minute. He got a spare tin plate for me and ordered the boys each to give me a little. I realized that he was their leader, their prefect, as they say at school. Some boys grumbled at having to divide with me, and if I hadn't been so hungry from traveling all day, I wouldn't have accepted a grain from those grumblers. Anyhow, we ate supper and then we prayed again and were dismissed."

Shinega listened with an open mouth. On the other side of the room, Zemwet was putting wood on the fire to make coffee. She suspected that her son was telling an interesting story, but could not hear him distinctly enough to follow it.

"Degemu," said Shinega, "you've been hiding your experiences from me. Did you even tell your mother?"

"No, of course not. This is the first time I've talked about those days with anyone. Such experiences are not interesting."

"To me they're very interesting. Tell me everything you remember."

"Well, every Saturday we used to sweep the mission buildings and smear the floors with manure to keep fleas out. We would take turns tending the mission cattle, frying our wheat, carrying in wood and straw . . . we had to carry it a long way. All that, we had to do. We even had to do women's chores, pound and grate false-banana root"—Shinega laughed—"but of all things I disliked at the mission, the worst was praying."

Shinega stopped laughing and looked uneasy.

"Yes, praying. In the morning when we got out of bed, we had to pray and go to Mass. Before and after breakfast, we had to pray. Before and after lunch, before and after supper, more praying. On Sunday between three and four in the afternoon we prayed what they called the 'benediction.' Sometimes I just wondered whether God really wanted men to be on their knees so much . . . or indeed, whether He listened at all."

"Leave that, let it be," said Shinega. "Now you are disgusted, thinking about your life there, aren't you?"

"Why? On the contrary, I enjoy these memories. If it hadn't been for the mission, I would have remained a villager all my life."

"Good. What else do you remember?"

"I've kept the most amusing thing for last. One morning, in the dining room, the biscuit reserved for the priest could not be found. The priest got angry and said, 'There is a thief among us! Until you turn him in to me, no one eats a thing, not even if you go hungry two whole days!'

"All the boys were frightened and decided to find the thief. They divided into three groups, each group to point out the boys who were suspected. One boy, a very tall skinny kid, for no reason I could understand told our group that he suspected *me!* I swore on the cross that I hadn't stolen the biscuit. The matter was taken to the father and he asked the skinny boy why he suspected me and the boy said: 'Last night when we left you in the dining room after saying good night, Degemu was the last one out. After he left, the door was locked. Therefore it is proved that he took your biscuit.'

"Fortunately, the boy who had really taken the biscuit stepped up and confessed and said I had nothing to do with it. That boy was such a good and innocent person . . . no one would have thought that he would pick up even a penny in the street, let alone steal. It was hard for the priest to accept his confession. 'My boy,' the father said, 'how could you, living in a mission, dare to steal the biscuit? Don't you know that that is a great sin?' 'Yes, father, I know it is a sin,' said the boy. 'But last night I didn't have enough fried wheat. I thought the biscuit was a leftover, so I took it and ate it.' The father, who was a very kind person, was impressed by the boy's innocence and by the courage he showed in confessing, so he didn't punish him. From then on, Welde Senbet was ordered to provide enough wheat for everyone. And so because of the thief, we all profited.

"As for me, I can never forget that tall skinny boy who suspected me for no reason at all."

"You have wonderful stories," said Shinega. "Tell me more."

"No, I don't remember others now. I'll tell you more as they come back to me."

The coffee was ready and the boys stopped talking to drink it.

16   DEGEMU GOES ABROAD

Degemu was to be at home only three days and then he would return to Addis Ababa. On the third day, Shinega asked Bala for a mule to see his friend off. When Shinega arrived at Atat, he removed the mule's bit and tethered its foreleg with a long rope tied to the fence. He entered the house and found Degemu and Zemwet talking. Zemwet greeted Shinega with the customary words: "How did your family spend the night?"

"Except for my sister, we are all right," said the boy. "But Theresa's sickness gets worse every day.

Mother had to stay up all night nursing her. Yesterday Mother planned to come and see Degemu, but now she is afraid to leave Theresa alone."

"May I share the girl's pain! She is so young to suffer so, too! May no unhappy tidings of her come to me!"

"God will not be cruel to her," said Shinega piously.

Zemwet resumed her conversation with her son.

"My son, you have finished your studies in Addis Ababa. I hear that young men with your education get money like scooping up dust. So why do you want to go beyond the sea?"

"I don't know myself, Mother. Something inside forces me. I am searching for something."

"For what? Can't it be found without going to the land of the whites?"

"I tell you, I myself don't know. My heart says go."

Shinega listened silently.

"Well, of course you pay no attention to me, but for all that, your mother thinks you should stay here. It would be much better for you not to go. I would be so happy if you would take a job, get married, and live like other honorable men live. But if you persist in going, then I hope you find what it is you are searching for."

Degemu looked at his watch. "I must leave now, Mother, before it is too late to catch the bus in Wolkitte."

"Well . . ." Zemwet's face became stiff with sadness. "Please leave me something as a keepsake, my son."

Degemu took a photograph from the inside pocket of his coat.

His mother held it to her lips and kissed it. "But this

is only paper," she said. "Give me the handkerchief with which you have wiped your sweat."

Degemu took out his handkerchief and looked at it. "This isn't very clean, Mother." He took out another, a new one. "Take this, it's better."

"No, the old one. It has your sweat on it and when I smell it, I'll remember you."

The people of the village, men, women, girls and boys, came one by one to see Degemu off. As he was going beyond the sea, no one could be sure that he would ever return safely. Maybe they would never see him again.

Tears came into Zemwet's eyes. Degemu kissed her, mounted his mule, and kicked his heels until the mule began to gallop. As his figure grew distant, the people of Atat went to their homes in sorrow.

Shinega, very worried about Theresa, hurried back to Wardéna.

17 THERESA DIES

All day and night the day Degemu left, Theresa weakened. Her headache turned into some other disease that no one could explain with certainty, and just before dawn the next morning she died.

Shinega had to go early to inform Zemwet. She was still asleep when he arrived, and he called to her.

"Shinega," Zemwet said, "why have you come so early? Can it be for a good reason?"

"Mother told me to tell you that Theresa is very weak."

"O God! She isn't dead yet, is she?"

"Not yet," the boy lied. "But how much longer she will live is uncertain."

Zemwet broke into tears, for she had loved Theresa very much. At once she dressed and they hurried to Wardéna.

The people in the neighborhood of Bala's house were very busy when Shinega and Zemwet arrived. Kartchea, the Fuga, was in the eucalyptus grove felling trees and cutting them up for firewood for the funeral. The women were behind the house at work with their toothed mallets pounding the root of the false-banana plant to feed the mourners. Others, inside and outside the house, were already wailing. Kerwagé lamented in this way:

"Theresa, my daughter, you who had not reached woman's years, you so young; who looked upon you with the evil eye and caused your death?

"Theresa, my daughter, O bride, will you be able to warm your new dwelling-place alone?

"Theresa, my daughter, is it true that you have said goodbye forever?

"Theresa, my daughter, I believe you are still alive, I say you still live, you are only sleeping."

And Zemwet joined her, crying:

"Death, die in your turn, you separate mother and child.

"Death, die in your turn, you separate husband and wife.

"Death, die in your turn, you separate the one who loves and the one who is loved.

"O hero, rise and gird yourself

"O hero, take your shield

"O hero, take down your spear.

88

"Death has come to your threshold
"Death has kidnapped your daughter
"Death has kidnapped your sister
"He has kidnapped your bride.
"O hero, rise in your anger!
"Pierce and kill your enemy!
"So that he will not come back
"So that he will not take away your sister
"So that he will not take away the beloved one."

Each mourner lamented according to his sorrow. Some pounded their ribs with their elbows and some slapped their faces. Some leaped high and fell back upon the earth.

As if Theresa would rise from death merely because ribs were pounded, faces were slapped, and men leaped high!

18   SHINEGA MARRIES

The death of her daughter caused Kerwagé great sorrow, and for half a year she lamented her. She shaved her head and never anointed it with butter. She lost weight until she could hardly be recognized. What consoled her was the sight of the little house that was being built for Shinega's marriage. That helped her forget her sorrow.

Time passed and three weeks before the wedding, children of the village began to come and sing and dance at Shinega's new house. They would come in the evening after supper and sing the *lala*-song. While the group clapped hands, a girl would chant:

In the woods to the east
  Lala shebo!
Who makes a noise?
  Lala shebo!
In the woods to the west
  Lala shebo!
Who rustles dry leaves?
  Lala shebo!
It is Shinega's footsteps
  Lala shebo!
As he looks for his beauty!
  Lala shebo!

The men of Ezha asked her hand
  Lala shebo!
She refused them all!
  Lala shebo!
Inor asked for her hand
  Lala shebo!
She said: I will never agree!
  Lala shebo!
When Shinega asked
  Lala shebo!
She said: He's the man for me!
  Lala shebo!

O bride, how happy you are!
  Lala shebo!
You have found a hard worker.
  Lala shebo!
O bride, how happy you are!
  Lala shebo!
He is of a good tribe.
  Lala shebo!
Don't show him to others!
  Lala shebo!

Keep him from the evil eye!
  Lala shebo!
Look at him only in secret!
  Lala shebo!

Listen, all you girls!
  Lala shebo!
Girls, spread the news!
  Lala shebo!
The disease of today
  Lala shebo!
Is what is called education.
  Lala shebo!
Since education came
  Lala shebo!
We are all old maids!
  Lala shebo!
The boys have left us
  Lala shebo!
The earth is untilled
  Lala shebo!
Education today
  Lala shebo!
Is no better than death!
  Lala shebo!
It takes away our boys
  Lala shebo!
Makes them strangers to their families.
  Lala shebo!

The children of Wardéna played and sang all night in Shinega's new house until the day of the wedding. Their noise kept the whole village awake, but as such play was customary, no one dared to tell them to be quiet.

For his wedding Shinega wore long white trousers and a white shirt that fell to his knees, over this his toga, and a brown hat that made him seem a different man. His father asked him to wear the shoes Yibgyeta had sent from Addis Ababa as a wedding gift, but he refused, saying: "I don't know how to wear shoes. I'll walk on the feet God gave me." The gathered wedding guests insisted that he put on the shoes, so finally he agreed to. His feet were large and the shoes seemed very small, but once he had them on, he would not remove them merely because they hurt. Then a student who was there began to laugh and said:

"Shinega, the trouble isn't that the shoes are too small."

"What's wrong then?"

"You have the right shoe on the left foot, and the left shoe on the right foot!"

Shinega took the shoes off and tried again, and this time they fitted well. There was much laughter and he felt embarrassed. To avoid making that mistake again, he tied a little string around the heel of the right-hand shoe.

Now he was ready to go fetch his bride. Four young men were to accompany him. They saddled their mules and toward mid-afternoon rode off. It was the end of the rainy season, the paths were muddy and slow, the rivers were high. When they came to a river-crossing, they had to unsaddle the mules and drive them into the water to force them to swim, then undress and swim across themselves carrying the saddles and their clothes. So delayed, it was midnight before they reached the bride's home.

When they were within hearing distance of the house, Shinega and his four companions broke into loud

song so that the wedding guests would know that they
had arrived and could come out to welcome them by
crying, as is customary, "il-il-ilil-il." Their mules were
taken to different houses in the village for the night,
and the young men were shown into the bride's home.
Her father was sitting on a mat in the *kakat* and the
mother was on a low stool near the fireplace. Naturally,
the bride was hidden behind a curtain near the partition
of the *derar*. Shinega kissed the bride's parents on the
right and left shoulder and then sat with his companions
at the places appointed for them. Then their feet were
washed and they were given food, beer, and honey-
mead. They were allowed to rest a few minutes. Then
the singers, young girls of the village, were called in.
The girls clapped their hands and one of them chanted:

> O bridegroom, rejoice!
> Lala shebo!
> Your bride is charming!
> Lala shebo!
> Your bride is a carafe
> Lala shebo!
> Take care not to break her!
> Lala shebo!

> O listen, bride, listen!
> Lala shebo!
> If they ask you, tell them
> Lala shebo!
> That you are of a good clan
> Lala shebo!
> Both father and mother of good family!
> Lala shebo!
> If they ask what you drink

Lala shebo!
Tell them fresh milk and honey!
Lala shebo!
If they ask what you eat
Lala shebo!
Tell them hump and chest of the bull!
Lala shebo!

A fast mule to ride
Lala shebo!
A fine toga to wear
Lala shebo!
If they can't afford these
Lala shebo!
Kick their shins and come home!
Lala shebo!

The night was spent in song and dancing and laughter. Early the next morning the bride's father made her a gift of two cows, and her mother blessed her. She was dressed in long white trousers, and over the trousers her dress. Now they covered her with a veil and helped her up on her mule. She broke into tears, as always happens, and still crying, kissed her parents goodbye.

Then a problem arose. The bride's girlfriends all wanted to accompany her to the wedding, but the Guragé law, at that time, permitted only eight attendants, in order to prevent unfair expense. The four young men with Shinega were instructed to choose the eight girls who were to go to Wardéna. They selected husky girls they thought would be able to walk well through mud. One of these was very black in color with a strong lush body. Above her waist she wore a sleeveless sweater that was swollen tight with her breasts. Her skirt was

slit above the knee and as she strode along, the young men could see her round thigh. She seemed tireless. The other girls were chocolate brown and also sturdy, and the little party made good time, singing and joking as they went.

The girls who accompanied the bride stayed with her one day and two nights in Shinega's new house, and left the second morning, as did the relatives and all the other guests. Shinega's house was now like an abandoned place, strangely silent after all the singing and dancing.

These two nights Shinega had slept in his parents' house, as was customary. On the evening of the third day, Bala said to him: "Now you must go to your own dwelling."

"Why tonight? Haven't I slept here well enough?"

"You must keep your bride company. She is a stranger and alone now that her friends have gone."

For some time Shinega refused, but finally he had to give in. His friends in the village knew, of course, that though he would be stubborn about it for a while, in the end he would spend the night with his bride. They came and hid in the darkness outside the door. Shinega addressed his bride for the first time.

"Girl, what is your name?"

She did not answer, for she was shy.

Shinega raised his voice:

"I am asking your name, girl!"

The boys outside laughed silently. One of them could not control his laughter, however, and broke into a guffaw that gave the game away. Shinega grabbed his spear and rushed out. The boys fled into the false-banana plantation; he chased them for some distance, then returned. He closed the door, leaned his spear against the wall, and went to sit behind the curtain with his bride. For several minutes he waited, listening to see if his friends would sneak back. Then he pulled off his trousers and his shirt, and prepared to sleep.

The girl, however, at once jumped up and fastened her toga and tied her belt around her waist, and went and stood near the central pillar.

Shinega knew her intentions. Angrily he said:

"Come here and lie down!"

The boys, back outside listening, burst into laughter, and then immediately ran off again, afraid that Shinega would come out with his spear.

Shinega ignored the boys and waited for his bride to join him. But she would not leave the pillar.

Without another word, he went and grabbed her and carried her behind the curtain.

Shinega blew out the light.

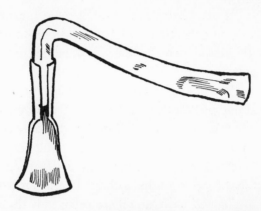

19 JUDGMENT AGAINST A THIEF

Kerwagé's preparations for the wedding—brewing of beer, baking of bread, melting of butter, pounding of salt and pepper—and then the three day's bustle of the wedding itself had tired her. With rest as her pretext, and a conversation as her purpose, she walked to Atat to visit Zemwet. Zemwet welcomed her as usual and then said:

"Kero, from now on, can there be anything you can possibly ask of God?"

Knowing Zemwet's drift, Kerwagé smiled and said: "What do you mean?"

"Now that your son is married, what else can you ask of life?"

"Is there anyone who is ever fully satisfied, Zemo? When one desire is attained, another is felt; when it is fulfilled, again one wants something else. My great wish now is to see my grandchildren."

"Well, you won't have to wait long. How old is Shinega now, by the way?"

"He is yesterday's child. I gave him life six years after you gave birth to Degemu. In other words, it was at the time when the law was decided forbidding bride money."

"You are right, he is very young. If my son Degemu had not gone to school, I would certainly have seen my grandchildren by now. But God did not will it."

"Has he written to you since going beyond the sea?"

"Nonsense. Even when he lived in Addis I would go five or six months without hearing a word. Do you think he will write any more often now that he is in the land of the whites?"

"It's strange, isn't it?"

"Isn't what strange?"

"That our boys go away to a land where they have neither parents nor relatives. Sometimes I think that education must change human nature."

"How can we who live in darkness say? Only God and the boys themselves can know that."

Zemwet, talking about her son, felt like crying, as usual. She believed that he would not come back alive. She changed the subject.

"How is your husband, Kero? We never see him around as we used to."

"He thinks there is now no one in the world greater

than he is, now that his son has become a man. He has someone to go with him to the assembly. He can rely upon him in a quarrel, and if no one in the village comes to the evening gathering, still he is not alone. My husband's heart is full."

"But why haven't we seen him of late? Is he so busy?"

"Since the wedding he has stayed at home and rested. Today, however, he went out early."

"Why should that be? Of course, he's a man of affairs."

"It's about our lost cow, Gwad's descendant. Like Gwad, she had the habit of wandering. One day she strayed away and we believed that she had been eaten by a hyena. But a man came and hinted that she was stolen."

"You have bad luck with white cows! Did the man say the cow is still alive?"

"No, he said she was slaughtered at Wolkitte. The hide is to be seen at the home of the thief."

While Kerwagé paid her visit, Bala traveled to investigate the theft of his white cow. He paid fifty Ethiopian dollars to the man who had informed him about her. He wanted to take the matter to the court at the Béro and have the thief imprisoned. But the thief, afraid of prison, appealed to the elders of his village. At first Bala insisted on court. The elders insisted on mediation. In the end, for among the Guragés it is the elders who win, it was agreed that Bala should nominate three elders, and the thief two, and that judgment should be rendered by these five men.

The house of the thief became a court. Many villagers came in to listen and to drink coffee. The elders

101

withdrew for consultation, and presently returned. The old man with the long beard and gray hair, the eldest of them all, pronounced their decision:

"May the tongue speak honestly! May God protect us from wrong judgment! May He make us strong and energetic that we may work for our living! May He shelter us from all evil! If this matter were taken to court," he went on, addressing the thief, "you would no doubt be fined heavily and also sent to prison. Since it was agreed that we, the elders, should judge, we have decided that you must give Bala two cows and his expenses, that is, the fifty dollars he had to pay his informant.

"You must do this within the week. If you fail to do so, we give Bala the right to take you into court."

The crowd was pleased with this judgment and dispersed voicing satisfaction. Bala went home, while the thief went to look for money.

20 SHINEGA'S BRIDE PREPARES TO VISIT HER PARENTS

Shinega's bride stayed behind her cloth curtain in their small house and had little to do. Sometimes she would roast coffee beans or churn milk. Village children often came to play the *wangena* game and sing the *lala-song* with her, so she was seldom alone. If she did happen to be alone, she would peep out a little hole she bored in the mud chinking between two boards of the side of the house, and watch people passing. If adults came to call on her, she would hide behind the curtain, as is customary until after the time of the *yeftezhubwar*, the bride's visit at her parents' home.

That was why, when Atshéwa came to the house one day, four months after the wedding, to see if the girl had changed, Shinega's bride covered her face with her toga.

"O bride, you don't have to veil yourself from me," Atshéwa said. "I've seen you a dozen times at the Béro market when you used to sell bamboo basket-tables."

She ignored him and kept her face covered.

"If you want me to buy you a little present, I'll get you a pair of anklets one of these days. Now pull that toga down from your face."

The girl was pleased with the promise of a gift, and unveiled herself. Nevertheless, she was too shy to look at Atshéwa's eyes.

Atshéwa found that she had changed a little. The small shaved place on her head, symbol of her virginity, had begun to fill in with hair. Her face had become more delicate. As she was not exposed to the sun, her skin had lightened. After observing her carefully for a few minutes, Atshéwa suggested a *wangena*-game, and asked her when she expected to visit her parents.

Shinega's bride calculated. "I have been behind the curtain four months," she said. "I'll go in one more month."

"Have you bought your new clothes for the trip yet?"

"I have the cotton and I'm spinning it."

Shinega came in and his bride ran behind the curtain and stayed there. Atshéwa said jokingly:

"Shinega, does your bride hide from you, too? I thought she only hid from others."

Shinega laughed. "She's just pretending. She pre-

tends to be shy because you are here. But if you weren't . . ."

"Then I better leave!"

Shinega asked him to stay longer, but Atshéwa said that he had to get back to his work, and he left them.

Shinega's bride spun the thread and the weft of the cloth for her new clothes. He told her that he could go to the market and buy ready-made clothes, but she said that those home-made are warmer. When the spinning was finished, there was the question of a weaver. Of the many weavers in Wardéna, the best was Buda Abu, and the bride of course wanted him. But Shinega knew from his mother that Abu had an evil eye and had made him sick when he was a baby. He feared that his bride's fingers, which had spun the cloth, would be bewitched by Abu's weaving.

When her clothes were ready, Shinega's bride returned to visit her parents.

21   DEGEMU WRITES FROM BEYOND THE SEA

While his bride was away, Shinega worked hard to get money with which they would live independently after her return. He bought coffee and sold it in Addis Ababa, and with his profits bought all manner of things needed in the country, and these he sold in the Béro market. After he had made several trips to Addis, his father said to him one day:

"Shinega, you should know Addis well by now. What is there that is strange and wonderful?"

"What is there in Addis that is not strange and wonderful? But of them all, these three are the greatest wonders: first, that people build houses on top of houses and live in the air. The second is what they call radio."

"Wait, my son," Bala interrupted. "How is it possible for people to live in houses on top of houses? Aren't the people who live in the upper house bothered by smoke from the lower one?"

"Father, the houses there don't have thatched roofs like ours. Their walls are stone and the roof is tin. They leave a special hole for the smoke to go out."

"Eh! Well, let that be, let it be. If I don't see such a house with my own eyes before God takes me, I'll never understand it. What about the thing called radio? What does it look like?"

"I can't understand radio myself. While people sit in a group, there are songs in Amharic or in the language of the whites, but when one looks around, one finds nothing and cannot tell whether the songs come from heaven or earth. In my opinion, it is devils singing and playing instruments. To add to your wonder, one sometimes even hears the *lala*-song."

"You are joking, my son!"

"I swear upon your hand, that nursed and fed me, that I tell you only the truth."

"Then you are right, it must be devils. It can't be anything else. In the name of the Father and of the Son and of the Holy Ghost."

Bala crossed himself.

"Well, and what is the third miracle?"

"The third is the airplane. When I see a machine made of iron and bigger than this house flying in the air, I ask myself why it doesn't fall down."

"I too have heard about the airplane. Before a kettle of water comes to a boil, one passes from Addis to

108

Djimma. And to walk from Addis to Djimma is a journey of two weeks and one arrives with swollen feet." Bala reflected for a moment. "There is nothing that time does not bring. In the old days there used to be a famous wizard who predicted many things and no one believed him, it seemed too fantastic. He used to say: 'I see crazy people, and horses without tails, and birds without souls.' And in our own time, all that has come to pass."

By the time his bride returned from her parents, already big with child, Shinega had accumulated nearly a hundred dollars. Bala now divided the land with him, the false-banana plantation and the coffee trees, as well as the eucalyptus grove, and gave him his share to cultivate. On that day Zemwet happened to come from Atat to see the bride and also to tell the family that she had received a letter from her son.

"Does he say that he is coming back?" asked Kerwagé.

"My friend, I'll believe he is coming back when he does come and I see his face. Nevertheless, it is true, he says that he is coming."

"What does his letter say?"

"As a student in my village read it and told it to me, it goes like this: 'Mother, don't think that I have forgotten you because I have not written before. I think of you all the time. Soon I'll be coming home although I have not found what I was looking for. Now I know that it does not exist.

" 'I like the life of the whites. Food and money are not scarce, as at home, but there is no friend or relative to whom one can open his heart. Every man lives for himself alone, not for others. Even if one loses a relative to death, the mourners do not lament and praise the dead man in song to console the bereaved. There is little difference between the young and the old. Everyone speaks no matter who is present, as if all were equals. When an elder comes into the house, he is not given one's chair; but when women come in, the men must rise to welcome them. At the homes to which I am invited, the husband sometimes serves the meal or drinks while his wife sits down. That astonishes me, of course, and I can't explain it. But here much is topsy-turvy.'"

Kerwagé spoke: "If the student read your son's letter truly, it is unbelievable. What kind of a country is it where the old and the young speak as equals, and the wife is seated while her husband serves the guests? If Shinega's father were so effeminate as *that* I would kick him and leave him today."

"Let the whites live as they want to, Kero. All I want is for my son to come back."

22 SHINEGA'S CHILD IS BORN

In the village of Wardéna it was evening. A fire of dry olive wood burned without smoke in the open fireplace in Shinega's house, flickering and casting shadows upon the round walls. Small calves, hungry for their mothers' udders, bawled in the stable. It was time for the cowherd to drive the village cattle home, and in Shinega's house, the lowing of the returning cattle could be heard.

While the maid-servant rinsed the kettle to prepare evening coffee, Shinega's wife lay on a mat near the fire warming herself. She did not feel well; she was far gone in pregnancy and the birth of the child was expected to-night or tomorrow. Shinega sat on the left side of the door, in the *kakat*, and smoked his big gourd water-pipe. As he silently sat there, he seemed to be pondering whether his wife would give birth to a daughter, or a son.

Naturally, Shinega hoped for a son . . .